THE Story Hour

COMPILED BY

ESTHER M. BJOLAND

1 9 6 2

STANDARD EDUCATION SOCIETY

CHICAGO

ART DIRECTOR
JOHN W. GATENBY, JR.

ASSOCIATE ARTISTS

WINIFRED GAILEN   HAROLD PETERSON
VANIS JONES   HELEN PRICKETT
BEA LEONARD   JAN ROSS
W. PAWLIGER   JANE SCOTT
RAYMOND WEBER

FOREWORD

Love of reading is a precious gift. But it is not something which is given to us by the wave of a magic wand, as the fairy godmothers were wont to bestow special gifts upon a fair prince or princess. The joys and rewards of reading are given to us by mothers and fathers who begin singing and reciting nursery rhymes long before we can talk. For it is these rhymes that bring delight to babies who are too young to know what most of the words mean.

This love of reading is developed by those parents who take the time for the seemingly endless demand to "Read me a story" when a child is two, three, four, and five years old. What an age to foster the love of reading! For then it is that the child is most eager to know things and is so susceptible to every sound and emotion. This is the time when his eyes can be opened to the beauty and wonder of flowers in bloom, clouds a-sailing in the sky, sunsets that glow, and stars that twinkle "like a diamond in the sky." This is the time, too, when his ears can be opened to the loveliness and the lilt and the rhythm of poetry and music, his mind to laughter, and his heart to a sympathetic understanding for all created things. Perhaps never again will a parent or guardian have an audience of such unbounded capacity.

The parent who has no time to recapture the pleasures of the story book world of *Peter Rabbit, Angus and the Ducks*, and the countless other stories that children love has denied himself one of the great satisfactions that come from being a parent. For he has missed the thrill and wonder that comes from seeing the response in his child's eyes as the adventures of some beloved storybook character are enjoyed over and over again.

Children live in two worlds—the real one and the one that exists in their imaginations. The mother or father who fails to understand the need of the imaginative world has failed to give his child that kind of fortress into which he may retreat again and again for reinforcements, as did the child who spent the day in *The Butterbean Tent*.

THE STORY HOUR is a collection of nursery rhymes, poems, and stories for children.

It was created to bring to little children nursery rhymes to which they will respond with every evidence of enjoyment, when these verses are read or sung to them. So full of bounce and skips and hops and jumps themselves, it is no wonder that they like *Hippity Hop to the Barber Shop* and *The Grand Old Duke of York*.

It was created to bring to little children the joy of hearing those "extraornery" names they like to let trickle off their tongues, such as those used in the story of *The White Goat*. It was made to satisfy their love of nonsensical and mirth-provoking words such as Laura E. Richards uses in *Mrs. Snipkin and Mrs. Wobblechin;* and to satisfy their love of adventure and surprise as found in the stories of *Mr. Groundhog Turns Around* and *The Trail of the Mad Moose*.

Each illustration was especially designed to enhance each rhyme, poem, and story and to amplify their meaning and to satisfy the young children's desires for action and detail.

Character development has become an accepted part of parental training of children. A major part of that development is to guide children into right attitudes. Parents can use books as a basis of fostering these attitudes and at the same time have fun doing it. Above all, however, they will find that the hours spent in the joy and delight of reading to their children will be the means of bestowing upon them that precious gift—the love of reading.

Esther M. Bjoland

ACKNOWLEDGEMENTS

We wish to express our appreciation and thanks to the publishers, authors, and periodicals listed below for their courteous cooperation, and to make the following acknowledgments.

MR. JAMES BRADY—for "Mr. Groundhog Turns Around" and to *Jack and Jill Magazine* in which Mr. Brady's story first appeared.

COWARD-McCANN, INC.—for "Gone Is Gone" from *Gone Is Gone* by Wanda Gág. Copyright 1935, by Wanda Gág. Reprinted by permission of Coward-McCann, Inc.

DOUBLEDAY & COMPANY, INC.—for "The Playhouse Key" and "The Ice Cream Man" from *Taxis and Toadstools* by Rachel Field. Copyright 1926 by Doubleday & Company, Inc.; and for "The White Goat" from *The Poppy Seed Cakes* by Margery Clark. Copyright 1924 by Doubleday & Company, Inc.; and for "Mr. Apple Names The Family" from *Mr. Apple's Family* by Jean McDevitt. Reprinted by permission of Doubleday & Company, Inc.; and for "Angus and the Ducks" from *Angus and the Ducks* by Marjorie Flack. Copyright 1930 by Doubleday & Company, Inc.

HARPER & BROTHERS—for "Park Play" from *I Live In The City* by James S. Tippett. Copyright 1927, Harper & Brothers.

LITTLE, BROWN & COMPANY—for "Mrs. Snipkin and Mrs. Wobblechin" and "The Umbrella Brigade" from *Tirra Lirra, Rhymes Old and New* by Laura E. Richards.

LOTHROP, LEE, AND SHEPHERD CO.—for "How Did He Do It" from *Through the Farmyard Gate* by Emilie Poulsson by permission of Lothrop, Lee, and Shepherd Co.

THE MACMILLAN COMPANY—for "Zebedee, Fisherman" from *Blue Teapot* by Alice Dalgleish by permission of The MacMillan Company.

AUDREY McKIM—for "The Trail of the Mad Moose" and to *Jack and Jill Magazine* in which Miss McKim's story first appeared.

THOMAS NELSON & SONS—for "Little Talk" from *That's Why* by Aileen Fisher. Thomas Nelson & Sons, New York. Used by permission of the publishers.

G. P. PUTNAM's SONS—for "Hiding" from *Everything and Anything*. Copyright 1925, 1926, 1927, by Dorothy Aldis. Courtesy of G. P. Putnam's Sons and "The Sprinkler" from *Everything and Anything* by Dorothy Aldis. Copyright 1927. Courtesy G. P. Putnam's Sons; and for "The Pancake" from *Tales From the Fjeld* by Peter Christian Asbjornsen and Jorgen Moe. Courtesy of G. P. Putnam's Sons.

WILLIAM R. SCOTT, INC.—for "Here Comes Daddy" from the book *Here Comes Daddy* with the permission of the publishers.

NANCY BYRD TURNER—for "The First Thanksgiving of All".

THE VIKING PRESS—for "The Butterbean Tent" from *Under the Tree* by Elizabeth Madox Roberts. Copyright 1922 by B. W. Huebsch, Inc., 1950 by Ivor S. Roberts. Reprinted by permission of The Viking Press, Inc., New York; and for "The Chinaberry Tree" from *Tag-Along-Tooloo* by Frances Clark Sayers. Illustrated by Helen Sewell. Copyright 1941 by Frances Clark Sayers and Helen Sewell. Copyright by permission of the Viking Press, Inc., New York.

YALE UNIVERSITY PRESS—for "Neighbors" by James Farrar from *Songs for Parents*. Used by permission of the publishers.

TABLE OF

CONTENTS

SMILING girls, rosy boys,
Come and buy my little toys;
Monkeys made of gingerbread,
And sugar horses painted red.

9

Rock-a-bye, baby, on the tree top!
When the wind blows
    the cradle will rock,
When the bough breaks
    the cradle will fall;
Down will come baby,
    cradle and all.

The north wind doth blow,
    We soon shall have snow,
And what will poor Robin do then?
    Poor thing!

He'll sit in a barn,
    To keep himself warm,
And hide his head under his wing.
    Poor thing!

10

One misty, moisty morning,
  When cloudy was the weather,
There I met an old man
  Clothed all in leather.
He began to compliment
  And I began to grin,
"How-do-you-do,"
  And "how-do-you-do,"
  And "how-do-you-do, again!"

11

Hippity hop to the barber shop
To buy a stick of candy;
One for you and one for me,
And one for sister Annie.

Hark, hark,
The dogs do bark,
Beggars are coming to town;
Some in jags,
Some in rags,
And some in velvet gowns.

I saw a ship a-sailing,
A-sailing on the sea;
And, oh! it was all laden
With pretty things for thee!

There were comfits in the cabin,
And apples in the hold;
The sails were made of silk,
And the masts were made of gold.

The four-and-twenty sailors
That stood between the decks,
Were four-and-twenty mice
With chains about their necks.

The captain was a duck,
With a packet on his back;
And when the ship began to move,
The captain said, "Quack! Quack!"

I had a little hobby-horse,
    And it was dapple gray,
It's head was made of pea-straw,
    Its tail was made of hay.
I sold it to an old woman
    For a copper groat;
And I'll not sing my song again
    Without another coat.

I'm going to Lady Washington's
To get a cup of tea
And five loaves of gingerbread,
So don't you follow me.

Where, oh, where
     has my little dog gone?
Oh, where, oh, where can he be?
With his tail cut short,
     And his ears cut long —
Oh, where, oh, where has he gone?

Pussy-cat, pussy-cat, where have you been?
I've been to London to look at the Queen.
Pussy-cat, pussy-cat, what did you there?
I frightened a little mouse under the chair.

Intery, mintery, cutery-corn,
Apple seed and apple thorn,
Wire, brier, limber-lock,
Three geese in a flock;
One flew east, and one flew west,
And one flew over the cuckoo's nest.

I have four brothers over the sea,
Perrie, Merrie, Dixie, Dominie,
And they each sent a present to me,
Petrum, Partrum, Paradise, Temporie,
Perrie, Merrie, Dixie, Dominie.

The Queen of Hearts,
She made some tarts,
All on a summer's day.

The Knave of Hearts,
He stole the tarts,
And took them clean away.

The King of Hearts
Called for the tarts,
And beat the Knave full sore.

The Knave of Hearts
Brought back the tarts,
And vowed he'd steal no more.

17

Helen
Prickett

"Bow, wow,"
Says the dog;
"Mew, mew,"
Says the cat.

"Grunt, grunt,"
Goes the hog;
And "squeak,"
Goes the rat.

"Chirp, chirp,"
Says the sparrow;

"Caw, caw,"
Says the crow.

"Quack, quack,"
Says the duck;
And what cuckoos say,
You know.

I asked my mother for fifty cents
To see the elephant jump the fence.
He jumped so high
He reached the sky
And never came back till the Fourth of July.

19

Here we go round the mulberry bush,
The mulberry bush, the mulberry bush,
Here we go round the mulberry bush,
So early in the morning.

This is the way we wash our hands,
We wash our hands, we wash our hands,
This is the way we wash our hands,
So early in the morning.

This is the way we dry our hands,
We dry our hands, we dry our hands,
This is the way we dry our hands,
So early in the morning.

This is the way we clap our hands,
We clap our hands, we clap our hands,
This is the way we clap our hands,
So early in the morning.

This is the way we warm our hands,
We warm our hands, we warm our hands,
This is the way we warm our hands,
So early in the morning.

Spring is showery,
     flowery, bowery;

Summer: hoppy,
     croppy, poppy;

Autumn: wheezy,
     sneezy, freezy;

Winter: slippy,
     drippy, nippy.

Ring a ring o'roses,
A pocketful of posies.
Tisha! Tisha!
We all fall down.

There was an old woman tossed up in a basket,
   Nineteen times as high as the moon;
And where she was going, I couldn't but ask it,
   For in her hand she carried a broom.

"Old woman, old woman, old woman," said I,
   "O whither, O whither, O whither so high?"
"To sweep the cobwebs off the sky!"
   "Shall I go with you?" "Aye, by and by."

The grand Old Duke of York
   He had ten thousand men,
He marched them up a very high hill
   And he marched them down again.
And when he was up he was up,
   And when he was down he was down,
And when he was only half way up
   He was neither up nor down.

UP
HALF WAY
DOWN

Apple Blossom

Lady Apple Blossom
    Just arrived in town,
Wears a light green bonnet
    And a snowy gown.

The pretty dress is —
    What do you think?
Five white petals
    Just touched with pink.

Kate Louise Brown

One March Day

As I was walking, one March day,
    Down the length of Blossom Street
Round me whirled a wind at play,
    And lifted me right off my feet.

English rhyme

24

I had a little nut tree; nothing would it bear,
   But a silver nutmeg and a golden pear.
The King of Spain's daughter came to visit me,
   And all was because of my little nut tree.
I skipped over water, I danced over sea,
   And all the birds in the air couldn't catch me.

The rain is raining all around,
   It falls on field and tree;
It rains on the umbrellas here,
   And on the ships at sea.

Robert Louis Stevenson

Rain, rain, go away,
   Come again another day;
Little Johnny wants to play.

26

Helen
Prickett

Mix a pancake,
Stir a pancake,
  Pop it in the pan;
Fry the pancake,
Toss the pancake,
  Catch it if you can.

Christina Georgina Rossetti

Little Tommy Tucker
  Sings for his supper.
What shall he eat?
  Brown bread and butter.

Helen
Prickett

27

Clouds

White sheep, white sheep,
  On a blue hill.
When the wind stops
You all stand still.
When the wind blows
You walk away slow.
White sheep, white sheep,
Where do you go?

Christina Georgina Rossetti

Lilies

I thought I saw white clouds, but no!—
  Bending across the fence,
  White lilies in a row!

Shiko 1665-1731

GATENBY

28

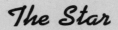

The Star

Twinkle, twinkle, little star
How I wonder what you are,
Up above the world so high,
Like a diamond in the sky!

When the blazing sun is set,
And the grass with dew is wet,
Then you show your little light,
Twinkle, twinkle, all the night.

Then the traveler in the dark
Thanks you for your tiny spark,
He could not see where to go
If you did not twinkle so.

In the dark blue sky you keep,
And often through my curtains peep,
For you never shut your eye
Till the sun is in the sky.

Jane Taylor

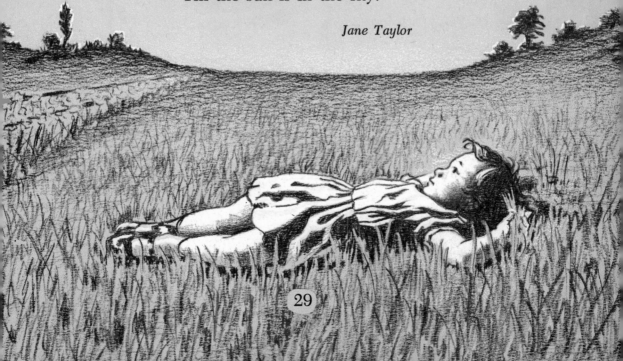

Little Dame Crump

Little Dame Crump
  With her little hair broom,
One morning was sweeping
  Her little bedroom;
When, casting her little
  Gray eyes on the ground,
In a dark little corner
  A penny she found.

"Odd Dobs!" cried the dame
  While she stared with surprise,
"How lucky I am!
  Bless my heart, what a prize!
To market I'll go,
  And a pig I will buy,
And little John Gubbins
  Shall make him a sty."

30

Jan Ross

She washed her face clean,
And put on her gown,
And locked up her house
And set off for the town
Where to market she went,
And a bargain she made;
For a little white pig
The penny she paid.

Then she carried the pig
To his nice little sty,
And made him a bed
Of clean straw, snug and dry.

Author unknown

31

Handy Pandy, Jack-a-dandy,
  Loves plum cake and sugar candy.
He bought some at a grocer's shop,
  And out he came, hop, hop, hop!

Bobby Shaftoe's gone to sea,
  Silver buckles on his knee;
He'll come back and marry me,
  Pretty Bobby Shaftoe!

Bobby Shaftoe's fat and fair,
  Combing down his yellow hair;
He's my love forevermore,
  Pretty Bobby Shaftoe.

Jan Ross

Tick, tock, tick, tock,
   Merrily sings the clock;
It's time for work,
   It's time for play,
So it sings throughout the day.
   Tick, tock, tick, tock,
Merrily sings the clock.

Once I saw a little bird
   Come hop, hop, hop;
So I cried, "Little bird,
   Will you stop, stop, stop?"
And went to the window
   To say "How do you do?"
But he shook his little tail
   And away he flew.

Time to Rise

A birdie with a yellow bill
    Hopped upon the window sill,
Cocked his shining eye and said:
    "Ain't you 'shamed, you sleepy-head?"

Robert Louis Stevenson

Bread and Milk for Breakfast

Bread and milk for breakfast,
    And woolen frocks to wear,
And a crumb for robin redbreast
    On the cold days of the year.

Christina Rossetti

Bed in Summer

In winter I get up at night
    And dress by yellow candle-light.
In summer, quite the other way,
    I have to go to bed by day.

I have to go to bed and see
    The birds still hopping on the tree,
Or hear the grown-up people's feet
    Still going past me on the street.

And does it not seem hard to you,
    When all the sky is clear and blue,
And I should like so much to play,
    To have to go to bed by day?

Robert Louis Stevenson

35

The Milkman's Horse

On summer mornings, when it's hot,
   The milkman's horse can't even trot,
But pokes along like this—
   Klip-klop, klip-klop, klip-klop.

But in the winter brisk,
   He perks right up and wants to frisk,
And then he goes like this—
   Klippty-klip, klippety-klip, klippty-klip.

Author Unknown

The Postman

The whistling postman swings along.
His bag is deep and wide,
And messages from all the world
Are bundled up inside.

The postman's walking up our street.
Soon now he'll ring my bell.
Perhaps there'll be a letter stamped
In Asia. Who can tell?

Author Unknown

Hiding

I'm hiding, I'm hiding,
And no one knows where!
For all they can see is my
    Toes and my hair.

And I just heard my father
Say to my mother—
"But, darling, he must be
    Somewhere or other.

"Have you looked in the inkwell?"
And Mother said, "Where?"
"In the INKWELL," said Father. But
    I was not there.

Then "Wait!" cried my mother—
"I think that I see
Him under the carpet." But
    It was not me.

Jan Ross

"Inside the mirror's
A pretty good place,"
Said Father and looked, but saw
    Only his face.

"We've hunted," sighed Mother,
"As hard as we could
And I AM so afraid that we've
    Lost him for good."

Then I laughed out aloud
And I wiggled my toes
And Father said—"Look, dear,
    I wonder if those

"Toes could be Benny's.
There are ten of them. See?"
And they WERE so surprised to find
    Out it was me!

Dorothy Aldis

39

A Kite

I often sit and wish that I
Could be a kite up in the sky,
And ride upon the breeze and go
Whichever way I chanced to blow.

Author Unknown

Here Comes Daddy

WINIFRED MILIUS

A boy named Peter had a cat named Finnigan.

One day just before supper Peter and Finnigan went out to the corner to watch for Peter's Daddy to come home. They looked up and down the street. They saw a lady with a baby carriage, a man sweeping leaves, two boys on a bicycle, and a little spotted dog.

BUT NO DADDY YET.

41

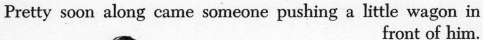

Pretty soon along came someone pushing a little wagon in
front of him.

Could this be Daddy
coming home?

No. It was a delivery
boy. He stopped and
took some groceries into
a red house and went
away.

NO DADDY YET.

A little truck came up the street.

Could this be Daddy
coming home?

No. It was a bread
truck. It stopped in front
of the grocery store and
the man delivered some
bread.

NO DADDY YET.

Around the corner came a car. A lady and dog were in it.

Could this be Daddy
coming home?

No. The car went by
without stopping. "P-s-s
-s-s-s-s-t!" said Finnigan
to the dog.

NO DADDY YET.

44

A big coal truck lum-
bered up the street.

Could this be Daddy
coming home?

No. The coal truck stopped at a house to deliver some coal.

Clankety, clankety.
Out rattled the coal into
barrels. Roll it away. Put
it in the cellar.

NO DADDY YET.

45

A great big moving van drove up and stopped.

Could this be Daddy
    coming home?

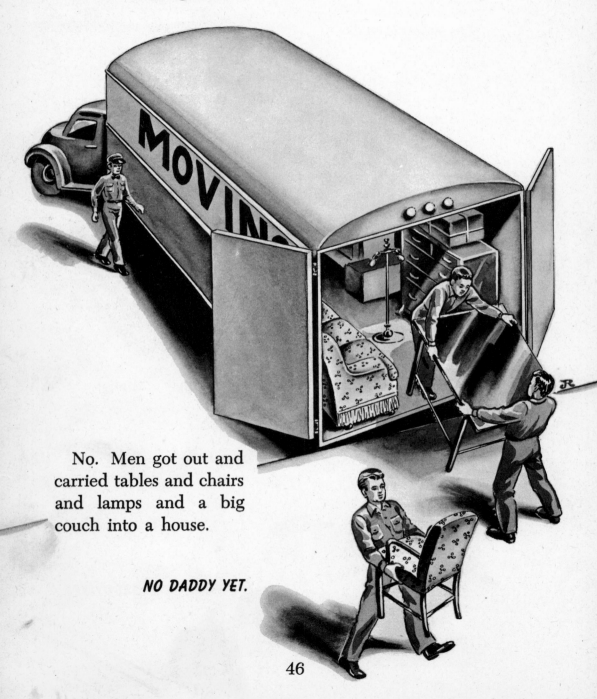

No. Men got out and
carried tables and chairs
and lamps and a big
couch into a house.

NO DADDY YET.

Up the street came
a truck squirting water
from its sides.

Could this be Daddy
    coming home?

No. It was a street sprinkling truck and water swish-sh-sh
-sh-shed all over the street.

NO DADDY YET.

47

Clop-clop, clop-clop came a horse and wagon.
Jingle, jangle went the bells on the wagon.

Could this be Daddy coming home?

No. It was the junk man carting off some scrap. He waved to Peter and Finnigan as he went by.

NO DADDY YET.

Then around the corner came a bus all full of people.

Could this be Daddy coming home?

The bus stopped and out got a little old man with an umbrella, a tall thin lady, a boy with a suitcase, and a man carrying a newspaper. "Here's Daddy, now!" shouted Peter.

Then Daddy took Peter's hand and they all walked home together.

The Chinaberry Tree

FRANCES CLARK SAYERS

Emily, Ann, Susan, and Virginia stood under the chinaberry tree. Talluluh stood there too. Talluluh was Ann's sister. They called her Tooloo for short, and short she was. She was five years old. She had only begun her growing.

Emily, Ann, Susan, and Virginia were talking about climbing the chinaberry tree. It was the largest chinaberry tree on Oleander Island. It was the largest chinaberry tree in the whole State of Texas. The trunk was smooth, which made it a hard tree to climb. But above the trunk there were many branches, easy to hold to, and because the tree looked like a great, round, open um-

brella it was called an umbrella chinaberry.

Emily, Ann, Susan, and Virginia planned a way to climb it. Emily stood on Virginia's shoulders. When she was safe, she pulled Ann up behind her. Susan followed. Then Virginia took off her sandals and walked up the tree, like a bug. Virginia had a brother. He had taught her how to climb trees. The girls were hidden in the thick leaves. There was not a shoe, sock, or bloomer to be seen. There stood Tooloo, all alone.

51

"Can I come too?" she said in a small voice.

"You're too little," said her sister Ann.

"It's too hard," said Virginia.

"We could lift her up," said Emily, "but it would be dangerous."

"Oh, Tooloo," said Susan, "you always want to do what we do! You always want to go where we go! Tag-along Tooloo, that's what you are." She made a sing-song of it:

Tag-along Too-loo Tag-along Too-loo Tag-along Too-loo Emily and Virginia sang it too. Tooloo cried.

"Susan," said Ann, "hush your mouth! Don't sing that to my sister." The singing stopped. Tooloo walked sadly toward the house. She went slowly around to the back door and into the kitchen. Aunt Melaynay was there, measuring out the grits. Aunt Melaynay was the cook. She was very wise, and told everyone what to do.

"Aunt Melaynay," said Tooloo, "the chilluns won't let me climb the chinaberry tree."

"Nevah min', Honey," said Aunt Melaynay. "Only li'l ole tomboys climb trees, anyhow. Don't you fret none."

But Tooloo thought it would be fun to climb that chinaberry tree. She thought and thought about it.

53

Emily, Ann, Susan, and Virginia had gone to a birthday party. Tooloo was too small to go. She hadn't even been invited. She stood under the chinaberry tree and looked up into the curve of its dark, leafy roof. Brody came down the street, scuffling through the grass which bordered the sidewalk. Brody lived in the alley. He was a little colored boy. He was Mary Brown's godchild, and he lived with Mary Brown. Mary Brown washed clothes for the whole neighborhood.

"Brody," said Tooloo, "could you help me climb this tree?"
"Sho' could," said Brody. "You jes' wait here." Brody ran off. He came back with a ladder. He put the ladder against the trunk of the tree. Then he took hold of Tooloo's hand, and she walked up the ladder, into the tree.

It was so easy!

She climbed from one branch to another until she was very near the top, and Brody could see nothing of her.

"Is you O. K., Tooloo?" he asked.

"Yes," she answered.

"Is there mosquitoes up there waitin' to bite you?"

"Nope," said Tooloo.

A voice rang through the air: "Brody! Godchile! Come on home here, an' bring in de clothes."

"Yas, Ma'am! I'se a-comin'," said Brody, and he grabbed up the ladder and ran down the street.

Varis

There was Tooloo in the chinaberry tree, but how was she
to get down? "I ought to be scared," she thought to herself.
But it was fun to be there, high, and hidden, and secret. She
peered through the leaves. Judge Rhodes was walking slowly
by, his green umbrella over his head. Tooloo called out some
lines she remembered from her favorite book:

> " 'Johnny Crow would dig and sow,
> Till he made a little garden.' "

The judge was astonished. Here, out of an empty street, someone was talking about gardens. The judged loved gardens. His own was famous for roses and strawberries. He stopped short. He swung his open umbrella down. He

looked up and down the street, at all the windows and galleries. There was no one to be seen. The windows were shuttered; the galleries were empty. "Bless my soul," he said aloud, and walked on, shaking his head. Tooloo laughed to herself. It was fun to astonish people.

All afternoon Tooloo sat in the chinaberry tree, astonishing people. Everyone who passed beneath the tree heard lines from "Johnny Crow's Garden" coming from he knew not where.

" 'And the lion
Had a green and yellow tie on,' "
shouted Tooloo above the head of kind Mrs. Lester, who walked with a cane. By four o'clock Tooloo's voice was almost gone. She was stiff from sitting in one place for so long a time.

TOOLOO

Aunt Melaynay came out. "Tooloo!" she shouted, and then: "Tooloo." Tooloo held very still, and said not a word. "Where is that chile?" she heard Aunt Melaynay muttering. "I'se phoned up everybody, and nobody's seen her."

Then Tooloo's mother came. "Tooloo," she called, "come here this minute. Are you hiding again?"

" 'Even the duckling
  Couldn't help chuckling'," said Tooloo in a cracked voice. Those lines were from "Johnny Crow's Party."

"Look there, Aunt Melaynay," said her mother. "She's up in that chinaberry tree."

Aunt Melaynay was furious. "You'se jes' like a ole cat!" she said. "You gits up high an' you can't git down. How'd you git up there, chile? How am I goin' to git you down?"

Then Aunt Melaynay thought of a ladder, and she went to fetch one. Tooloo's mother climbed up the ladder and reached up in the tree for Tooloo.

"Tooloo," she said, "why didn't you answer Aunt Melaynay when she called you?"

"She needs a whuppin'," said Aunt Melaynay, "a good whuppin'." Aunt Melaynay was always talking about "whuppin's," but no one could remember ever getting one from her.

"Poh li'l' baby," said Aunt Melaynay, "she's so tired she can't stan'."

Tooloo was tired. She was stiff and sore as well. She could hardly speak above a whisper.

"Poh li'l' chile," said Aunt Melaynay. "She needs a good whuppin'. But first I'm goin' to gib' her her suppah, and put her to bed.

Tooloo threw her arms around Aunt Melaynay's neck, and laid her head down on Aunt Melaynay's shoulder.

When Ann came home from the birthday party, she went to Tooloo's room. She had a piece of birthday cake to give her. Tooloo looked at her and smiled. "I climbed the chinaberry tree," she said.

In the Meadow

In the meadow — what is in the meadow?
Bluebells, buttercups, meadowsweet,
And fairy rings for children's feet,
In the meadow.

Christine G. Rossetti

Park Play

Every morning
  I can play
In the park
  Across the way.

I can run
  And I can shout.
I am glad
  When I come out.

James S. Tippett

63

A Fairy Voyage

If I were just a fairy small,
I'd take a leaf and sail away,
I'd sit astride the stem and guide
It straight to Fairyland and stay.

Unknown

64

Gone Is Gone

by WANDA GAG

This is an old, old story which my grandmother told me when I was a little girl. When she was a little girl her grandfather had told it to her, and when he was a little peasant boy in Bohemia, his mother had told it to him. And where she heard it, I don't know, but you can see it is an old, old story, and here it is, the way my grandmother used to tell it. It is called

GONE IS GONE and it is the story of a man who wanted to do housework. This man, his name was Fritzl—his wife, her name was Liesi. They had a little baby, Kinndli by name, and Spitz who was a dog.

They had one cow, two goats, three pigs, and of geese they had a dozen. That's what they had.

They lived on a patch of land, and that's where they worked.

Fritzl had to plow the

ground, sow the seeds and hoe

the weeds. He had to
cut the hay and

rake it too, and stack it up in
bunches in the

sun. The man worked hard, you see, from day to day.

Liesi had the house to clean,

the soup to cook,

the butter to churn,

the barn yard and
the baby to care for.

She, too, worked hard each day as you can plainly see.

They both worked hard, but Fritzl always thought that he worked harder. Evenings when he came home from the field he sat down, mopped his face with his big red handkerchief, and said: "Hu! How hot it was in the sun today, and how hard I did work. Little do you know, Liesi, what a man's work is like, little do you know! Your work now, 'tis nothing at all."

"'Tis none too easy," said Liesi.

"None too easy!" cried Fritzl. "All you do is to putter and potter around the house a bit — surely there's nothing hard about such things."

"Nay, if you think so," said Liesi, "we'll take it turn and turn about tomorrow. I will do your work, you can do mine. I will go out in the fields and cut the hay, you can stay here at home and putter and potter around. You wish to try it—yes?"

Fritzl thought he would like that well enough—to lie on the grass and keep an eye on his Kinndli-girl, to sit in the cool shade and churn, to fry a bit of sausage and cook a little soup. Ho! That would be easy! Yes, yes, he'd try it.

Well, Liesi lost no time the next morning. There she was at peep of day, striding out across the fields with a jug of water in her hand and the scythe over her shoulder.

And Fritzl, where was he? He was in the kitchen, frying a string of juicy sausages for his breakfast. There he sat, holding the pan over the fire, and as the sausage was sizzling and frizzling in the pan, Fritzl was lost in pleasant thoughts.

"A mug of cider now," that's what he was thinking. "A mug of apple cider with my sausage—that would be just the thing."

No sooner thought than done.

Fritzl set the pan on the edge of the fire place, and went down into the cellar where there was a big barrel full of cider. He pulled the bung from the barrel and watched the cider spurt into his mug, sparkling and foaming so that it was a joy to see.

But Hulla! What was that noise up in the kitchen—such a scuffle and clatter! Could it be that Spitz-dog after the sausages? Yes, that's what it was, and when Fritzl reached the top of the stairs, there he was, that dog, dashing out of the kitchen door with the string of juicy sausages flying after him.

Fritzl made for him, crying, "Hulla! Hulla! Hey, hi, ho, hulla!" But the dog wouldn't stop. Fritzl ran, Spitz ran too. Fritzl ran fast, Spitz ran faster, and the end of it was that the dog got away and our Fritzl had to give up the chase.

"Na, na! What's gone is gone," said Fritzl, shrugging his shoulders. And so he turned back, puffing and panting, and mopping his face with his big red handkerchief.

But the cider, now! Had he put the bung back in the barrel? No, that he hadn't, for he was still holding the bung in his fist.

With big fast steps Fritzl hurried home, but it was too late, for look! The cider had filled the mug and had run all over the cellar besides.

Fritzl looked at the cellar full of cider. Then he scratched his head and said, "Na, na! What's gone is gone."

Well, now it was high time to churn the butter. Fritzl filled the churn with good rich cream, took it under a tree and began to churn with all his might. His little Kinndli was out there too, playing Moo-cow among the daisies. The sky was blue, the sun right gay and golden, and the flowers, they were like angels' eyes blinking in the grass.

"This is pleasant now," thought Fritzl, as he churned away. "At last I can rest my weary legs. But wait! What about the cow? I've forgotten all about her and she hasn't had a drop of water all morning, poor thing."

With big fast steps Fritzl ran to the barn, carrying a bucket of cool fresh water for the cow. And high time it was, I can tell you, for the poor creature's tongue was hanging out of her mouth with the long thirst that was in her. She was hungry too, as a man could well see by the looks of her, so Fritzl took her from the barn and started off with her to the green grassy meadow.

But wait! There was that Kinndli to think of—she would surely get into trouble if he went out to the meadow. No, better not take the cow to the meadow at all. Better keep her nearby on the roof. The roof? Yes, the roof!

Fritzl's house was not covered with shingles or tin or tile—it was covered with moss and sod, and a fine crop of grass and flowers grew there.

To take the cow up on the roof was not so hard as you might think, either. Fritzl's house was built into the side of a hill. Up the little hill, over a little shed, and from there to the green grassy roof. That was all there was to do and it was soon done.

The cow liked it right well up there on the roof and was soon munching away with a will, so Fritzl hurried back to his churning.

But Hulla! Hui! What did he see there under the tree? Kinndli was climbing up on the churn—the churn was tipping! spilling! falling! and now, there on the grass lay Kinndli, all covered with half-churned cream and butter.

"So that's the end of our butter," said Fritzl, and blinked and blinked his blue eyes. Then he shrugged his shoulders and said, "Na, na! What's gone is gone."

He picked up his dripping Kinndli and set her in the sun to dry. But the sun, now! It had climbed high up into the heavens. Noontime it was, no dinner made, and Liesi would soon be home for a bite to eat.

With big fast steps Fritzl hurried off to the garden. He gathered potatoes and onions, carrots and cabbages, beets and beans, turnips, parsley and celery.

"A little of everything, that will make a good soup," said Fritzl as he went back to the house, his arms so full of vegetables that he could not even close the garden gate behind him.

He sat on a bench in the kitchen and began cutting and paring away. How the man did work, and how the peelings and parings did fly!

But now there was a great noise above him. Fritzl jumped to his feet.

"That cow," he said, "she's sliding around right much up there on the roof. She might slip off and break her neck."

Up on the roof went Fritzl once more, this time with loops of heavy rope. Now listen carefully, and I will tell you what he did with it. He took one end of the rope and tied it around the cow's middle. The other end of the rope he dropped down the chimney and this he pulled through the fireplace in the kitchen below.

And then? And then he took the end of the rope which was hanging out of the fireplace and tied it around his own middle with a good tight knot. That's what he did.

"Oh, yo! Oh ho!" he chuckled. "That will keep the cow from falling off the roof." And he began to whistle as he went on with his work.

He heaped some sticks on the fireplace and set a big kettle of water over it.

"Na, na!" he said. "Things are going as they should at last, and we'll soon have a good big soup! Now I'll put the vegetables in the kettle—"

And that he did.

"And now I'll put in the bacon—"

And that he did too.

"And now I'll light the fire—"

But that he never did, for just then, with a bump and a thump, the cow slipped over the edge of the roof after all; and Fritzl—well, he was whisked up into the chimney and there he dangled, poor man, and couldn't get up and couldn't get down.

Before long, there came Liesi home from the fields with the water jug in her hand and the scythe over her shoulder.

But Hulla! Hui! What was that hanging over the edge of the roof? The cow? Yes, the cow, and half-choked she was, too, with her eyes bulging and her tongue hanging out.

Liesi lost no time. She took her scythe—and ritsch! rotsch! —the rope was cut, and there was the cow wobbling on her four legs, but alive and well, heaven be praised!

Now Liesi saw the garden with its gate wide open. There were the pigs and the goats and all the geese too. They were full to bursting, but the garden, alas! was empty.

Liesi walked on, and now what did she see? The churn up-turned, and Kinndli there in the sun, stiff and sticky with dried cream and butter.

Liesi hurried on. There was Spitz-dog on the grass. He was full of sausages and looked none too well.

Liesi looked at the cellar. There was the cider all over the floor and halfway up the stairs besides.

Liesi looked in the kitchen. The floor! It was piled high with peelings and parings, and littered with dishes and pans.

At last Liesi saw the fireplace. Hu! Hulla! Hui! What was that in the soup-kettle? Two arms were waving, two legs were kicking, and a gurgle, bubbly and weak-like, was coming up out of the water.

"Na, na! What can this mean?" cried Liesi. She did not know (but we do —yes?) that when she saved the cow outside, something happened to Fritzl. Yes, as soon as the cow's rope was cut, Fritzl, poor man, he dropped down the chimney and crash! splash! fell right into the kettle of soup in the fireplace.

Liesi lost no time. She pulled at the two arms and tugged at the legs— and there, dripping and spluttering, with a cabbage-leaf in his hair, celery in his pocket, and a sprig of parsley over one ear, was her Fritzl.

"Na, na, my man!" said Liesi. "Is that the way you keep house—yes?"

"Oh Liesi, Liesi!" sputtered Fritzl. "You're right—that work of yours, 'tis none too easy."

"'Tis a little hard at first," said Liesi, "but tomorrow, maybe, you'll do better."

"Nay, nay!" cried Fritzl. "What's gone is gone, and so is my housework from this day on. Please, please, my Liesi— let me go back to my work in the fields, and never more will I say that my work is harder than yours."

"Well then," said Liesi, "if that's how it is, we surely can live in peace and happiness for ever and ever."

And that they did.

The Pancake

By ASBJORNSEN and MOE

Jane Scott

Once on a time there was a goody who had seven hungry bairns, and she was frying a pancake for them. It was a sweet-milk pancake, and there it lay in the pan bubbling and frizzling so thick and good, it was a sight for sore eyes to look at. And the bairns stood round about, and the goodman sat by and looked on.

"Oh, give me a bit of pancake, mother, dear; I am so hungry," said one bairn.

"Oh, darling mother," said the second.

"Oh, darling, good mother," said the third.

"Oh, darling, good, nice mother," said the fourth.

"Oh, darling, good, nice, pretty mother," said the fifth.

"Oh, darling, good, nice, pretty, clever mother," said the sixth.

"Oh, darling, good, nice, pretty, clever, sweet mother," said the seventh.

So they begged for the pancake all round, the one more prettily than the other; for they were so hungry and so good.

83

"Yes, yes, bairns, only bide a bit till it turns itself," — she ought to have said, "till I can get it turned,"—"and then you shall all have some — a lovely sweet-milk pancake; only look how fat and happy it lies there."

When the pancake heard that it got afraid, and in a trice it turned itself all of itself, and tried to jump out of the pan; but it fell back into it again t'other side up, and so when it had been fried a little on the other side too, till it got firmer in its flesh, it sprang out on the floor, and rolled off like a wheel through the door and down the hill.

"Helloa! Stop, pancake!" and away went the goody after it, with the frying-pan in one hand and the ladle in the other, as fast as she could, and her bairns behind her, while the goodman limped after them all.

"Hi, won't you stop? Seize it. Stop, pancake," they all screamed out, one after the other, and tried to catch it on the run and hold it; but the pancake rolled on and on, and in the twinkling of an eye it was so far ahead that they couldn't see it, for the pancake was faster on its feet than any of them.

So when it had rolled a while it met a man.

"Good day, pancake," said the man.

"God bless you, Manny Panny!" said the pancake.

"Dear pancake," said the man, "don't roll so fast; stop a little and let me eat you."

"When I have given the slip to Goody Poody, and the good-man, and seven squalling children, I may well slip through your fingers, Manny Panny," said the pancake, and rolled on and on till it met a hen.

"Good day, pancake," said the hen.

"The same to you, Henny Penny," said the pancake.

"Pancake, dear, don't roll so fast, but bide a bit and let me eat you up," said the hen.

"When I have given the slip to Goody Poody, and the goodman, and seven squalling children, and Manny Panny, I may well slip through your claws, Henny Penny," said the pancake, and so it rolled on like a wheel down the road.

Just then it met a cock.

"Good day, pancake," said the cock.

"The same to you, Cocky Locky," said the pancake.

"Pancake, dear, don't roll so fast, but bide a bit and let me eat you up."

Jane Scott

"When I have given the slip to Goody Poody, and the good-man, and seven squalling children, and to Manny Panny, and Henny Penny, I may well slip through your claws, Cocky Locky," said the pancake, and off it set rolling away as fast as it could; and when it had rolled a long way it met a duck.

"Good day, pan-cake," said the duck.

"The same to you, Ducky Lucky."

"Pancake, dear, don't roll away so fast; bide a bit and let me eat you up."

"When I have given the slip to Goody Poody, and the good-man, and seven squalling children, and Manny Panny, and Henny Penny, and Cocky Locky, I may well slip through your fingers, Ducky Lucky," said the pancake, and with that it took to rolling and rolling faster than ever; and when it had rolled a long, long while, it met a goose.

"Good day, pancake," said the goose.

"The same to you, Goosey Poosey."

"Pancake, dear, don't roll so fast; bide a bit and let me eat you up."

"When I have given the slip to Goody Poody, and the good-man, and seven squalling children, and Manny Panny, and Henny Penny, and Cocky Locky, and Ducky Lucky, I can well slip through your feet, Goosey Poosey," said the pancake, and off it rolled.

So when it had rolled a long, long way farther it met a gander.

"Good day, pancake," said the gander.

"The same to you, Gander Pander," said the pancake.

"Pancake, dear, don't roll so fast; bide a bit and let me eat you up."

"When I have given the slip to Goody Poody, and the goodman, and seven squalling children, and Manny Panny, and Henny Penny, and Cocky Locky, and Ducky Lucky, and Goosey Poosey, I may well slip through your feet, Gander Pander," said the pancake, which rolled off as fast as ever.

So when it had rolled a long, long, long time, it met a pig.

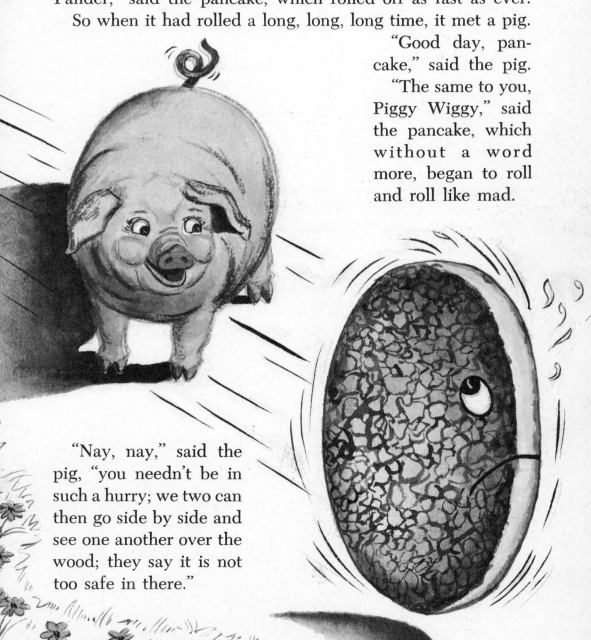

"Good day, pancake," said the pig.

"The same to you, Piggy Wiggy," said the pancake, which without a word more, began to roll and roll like mad.

"Nay, nay," said the pig, "you needn't be in such a hurry; we two can then go side by side and see one another over the wood; they say it is not too safe in there."

The pancake thought there might be something in that, and so they kept company. But when they had gone awhile, they came to a brook. As for Piggy, he was so fat he swam safe across, it was nothing to him; but the poor pancake couldn't get over.

"Seat yourself on my snout," said the pig, "and I'll carry you over."

So the pancake did that.

"Ouf, ouf," said the pig, and swallowed the pancake at one gulp; and then, as the poor pancake could go no farther, why—this story can go no farther either.

Tale of Peter Rabbit

BEATRIX POTTER

Once upon a time there were four little Rabbits, and their names were—

Flopsy,

Mopsy,

Cotton-tail,

and Peter.

They lived with their Mother in a sandbank, underneath the root of a very big fir-tree.

"Now, my dears," said old Mrs. Rabbit one morning, "you may go into the fields or down the lane, but don't go into Mr. McGregor's garden; your Father had an accident there; he was put in a pie by Mrs. McGregor. Now run along, and don't get into mischief; I am going out."

Then old Mrs. Rabbit took a basket and her umbrella, and went through the wood to the baker's. She bought a loaf of brown bread and five currant buns.

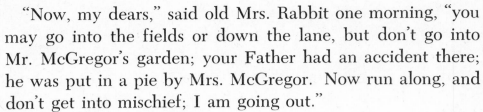

Flopsy, Mopsy, and Cotton-tail, who were good little bunnies, went down the lane to gather blackberries; but Peter, who was very naughty, ran straight away to Mr. McGregor's garden, and squeezed under the gate!

First he ate some lettuces and some French beans; and then he ate some radishes; and then, feeling rather sick, he went to look for some parsley.

But round the end of a cucumber frame, whom should he meet but Mr. McGregor!

Mr. McGregor was on his hands and knees planting out young cabbages, but he jumped up and ran after Peter, waving a rake and calling out, "Stop thief!"

Peter was most dreadfully frightened; he rushed all over the garden, for he had forgotten the way back to the gate.

He lost one of his shoes among the cabbages, and the other shoe amongst the potatoes.

After losing them, he ran on four legs and went faster, so that I think he might have got away altogether if he had not unfortunately run into a gooseberry net, and got caught by the large buttons on his jacket. It was a blue jacket with brass buttons, quite new.

Peter gave himself up for lost, and shed big tears; but his sobs were overheard by some friendly sparrows, who flew to him in great excitement, and implored him to exert himself.

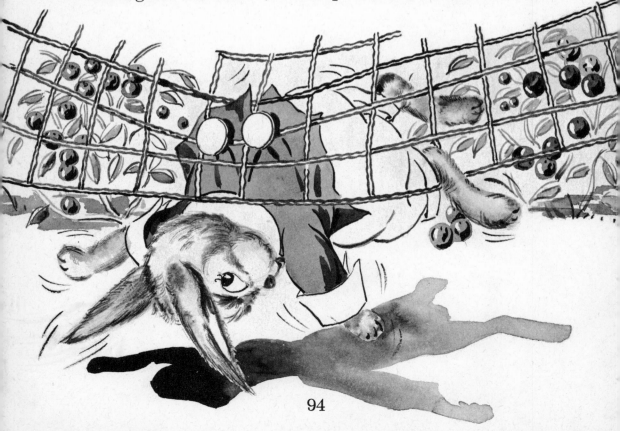

Mr. McGregor came up with a sieve, which he intended to pop upon the top of Peter; but Peter wriggled out just in time, leaving his jacket behind him. And rushed into the tool-shed, and jumped into a can. It would have been a beautiful thing to hide in, if it had not had so much water in it.

Mr. McGregor was quite sure that Peter was somewhere in the toolshed, perhaps hidden underneath a flower-pot. He began to turn them over carefully, looking under each.

Presently Peter sneezed—"Kertyschoo!" Mr. McGregor was after him in no time, and tried to put his foot upon Peter, who jumped out of the window, upsetting three plants. The window was too small for Mr. McGregor, and he was tired of running after Peter. He went back to his work.

Peter sat down to rest; he was out of breath and trembling with fright, and he had not the least idea which way to go. Also he was very damp with sitting in that can.

After a time he began to wander about, going lippity-lippity-not very fast, and looking all around.

He found a door in a wall; but it was locked, and there was no room for a fat little rabbit to squeeze underneath.

An old mouse was running in and out over the stone door-step, carrying peas and beans to her family in the wood. Peter asked her the way to the gate, but she had such a large pea in her mouth that she could not answer. She only shook her head at him. Peter began to cry.

Then he tried to find his way straight across the garden, but he became more and more puzzled. Presently, he came to a pond where Mr. McGregor filled his watercans. A white cat was staring at some goldfish; she sat very, very still, but now and then the tip of her tail twitched as if it were alive. Peter thought it best to go away without speaking to her; he had heard about cats from his cousin, little Benjamin Bunny.

He went back towards the tool-shed, but suddenly, quite close to him, he heard the noise of a hoe—scr-r-ritch, scratch, scratch, scritch. Peter scuttered underneath the bushes. But presently, as nothing happened, he came out, and climbed upon a wheel-barrow, and peeped over. The first thing he saw was Mr. McGregor hoeing onions. His back was turned towards Peter, and beyond him was the gate!

Peter got down very quietly off the wheel-barrow, and started running as fast as he could go, along a straight walk behind some black-currant bushes.

Mr. McGregor caught sight of him at the corner, but Peter did not care. He slipped underneath the gate, and was safe at last in the wood outside the garden.

Mr. McGregor hung up the little jacket and the shoes for a scare-crow to frighten the blackbirds.

Peter never stopped running or looked behind him till he got home to the big fir-tree.

He was so tired that he flopped down upon the nice soft sand on the floor of the rabbit hole, and shut his eyes. His mother was busy cooking; she wondered what he had done with his clothes. It was the second little jacket and pair of shoes that Peter had lost in a fortnight!

I am sorry to say that Peter was not very well during the evening.

His mother put him to bed and made some camomile tea; and she gave a dose of it to Peter!

"One table-spoonful to be taken at bedtime."

But Flopsy, Mopsy, and Cotton-tail had bread and milk and blackberries for supper.

Where Go the Boats

Dark brown is the river;
   Golden is the sand.
It flows along forever,
   With trees on either hand.

Green leaves a-floating,
   Castles of the foam,
Boats of mine a-boating—
   Where will all come home?

On goes the river
   And out past the mill,
Away down the valley,
   Away down the hill.

Away down the river,
   A hundred miles or more,
Other little children
   Shall bring my boats ashore.

Robert Louis Stevenson

Little Talk

Don't you think it's probable
that beetles, bugs, and bees
talk about a lot of things—
you know, such things as these:

The kind of weather where they live
in jungles tall with grass
and earthquakes in their villages
whenever people pass!

Of course, we'll never know if bugs
talk very much at all,
because our ears are far too big
for talk that is so small.

Aileen Fisher

101

The Umbrella Brigade

"Pitter patter!" falls the rain
On the schoolroom windowpane.
Such a plashing! such a dashing!
Will it e'er be dry again?
Down the gutter rolls a flood,
And the crossing's deep in mud;
And the puddles! oh, the puddles
Are a sight to stir one's blood!

Chorus.   But let it rain
        Tree-toads and frogs
        Muskets and pitchforks,
        Kittens and dogs!
        Dash away! plash away!
        Who is afraid?
        Here we go,
        The Umbrella Brigade!

Pull the boots up to the knee!
Tie the hoods on merrily!
Such a hustling! such a jostling!
Out of breath with fun are we.
Clatter, clatter, down the street,
Greeting every one we meet,
With our laughing and our chaffing,
Which the laughing drops repeat.

Chorus.　　　So let it rain
　　　　　　Tree-toads and frogs,
　　　　　　Muskets and pitchforks,
　　　　　　Kittens and dogs!
　　　　　　Dash away! plash away!
　　　　　　Who is afraid?
　　　　　　Here we go,
　　　　　　The Umbrella Brigade!

Laura E. Richards

103

What Robin Told

How do robins build their nests?
  Robin Redbreast told me—
First a wisp of yellow hay
In a pretty round they lay;
Then some shreds of downy floss,
Feathers too, and bits of moss,
Woven with a sweet, sweet song,
This way, that way, and across;
  That's what Robin told me.

Where do robins hide their nests?
  Robin Redbreast told me—
Up among the leaves so deep,
Where the sunbeams rarely creep.
Long before the winds are cold,
Long before the leaves are gold,
Bright-eyed stars will peep and see
Baby robins—one, two, three;
  That's what Robin told me.

George Cooper

The White Goat

By MARGERY CLARK

One fine Saturday morning Andrewshek's Auntie Katushka said, "Andrewshek, I must go to market and buy a goat."

Andrewshek was playing in the garden. He had pulled out some of the feathers from his fine feather bed and had put them in his hair. He looked very funny.

As Andrewshek's Auntie Katushka went out of the gate to go to market, Andrewshek said, "May I go with you, Auntie Katushka?"

"No, Andrewshek!" said his Auntie Katushka. "You must stay at home. Please watch to see that the dog does not open the gate and let the chickens and the cat run out into the road."

"Yes, indeed, I will watch to see that the dog does not open the gate. And I will be sure that the chickens and the cat do not run out into the road."

Then Auntie Katushka, in her bright shawl, hurried off to market. But all Andrewshek really did was to swing backward and forward and backward and forward on the dark green gate.

Andrewshek loved to swing backward and forward on the gate just as much as he loved to bounce up and down on his fine feather bed.

At the market Auntie Katushka saw a white goat. The white
goat had a long beard and a short tail. "That is just the goat I
want!" said Auntie Katushka.

"White Goat!" said Auntie Katushka, "I am going to take
you home with me to Andrewshek."

"Who is Andrewshek?" said the goat.

"Andrewshek is a little boy who lives across the tracks and up the hill, in a little house with a dark green gate. Andrewshek loves to swing backward and forward and backward and forward on the dark green gate."

"I would not be surprised if Andrewshek was swinging backward and forward on the green gate now," said the goat to herself. "I think I'll run ahead and see."

She galloped off.

"Stop, White Goat!" cried Aunt Katushka. "Stop!"

But the goat did not stop. She ran faster and faster, across the tracks and up the hill until she came to the little house with the dark green gate. Andrewshek was swinging backward and forward and backward and forward on the dark green gate. The chickens and the cat had long before run out into the road.

111

"How do you do, Andrewshek?" said the white goat.

"How do you do, White Goat?" said Andrewshek. "Where are you going?"

"No further!" said the white goat. "I belong to your Auntie Katushka."

"Where is my Auntie Ka-tushka?" said Andrewshek.

"I ran away from her, across the tracks and up the hill; and here I am!" said the goat.

"Won't Auntie Katushka be surprised when she sees you here!" said Andrewshek.

"I think I will hide!" said the white goat. She ran behind the little house.

Andrewshek's Aunt Katushka, in her bright shawl, came hurrying up the hill.

"Andrewshek, I bought a sweet white goat at the market to give us milk for our poppy seed cakes. She ran away and so we cannot have any poppy seed cakes today. I wonder how we can find her!"

"Ha! ha! ha!" the sweet white goat called out. She had

climbed to the top of the roof where she could look down on Andrewshek and Auntie Katushka.

"Come down from the roof, you naughty White Goat!" said Auntie Katushka. The goat shook her head.

"Please come down!" said Andrewshek. "And I will give you a big poppy seed cake."

"I do not like poppy seed cakes," said the naughty white goat.

"What shall we do?" said Andrewshek.

Andrewshek's Auntie Katushka went into the house and took off her bright shawl. She put on her apron.

She washed some turnips and some parsnips, two onions and four carrots for the soup. Then she cut the green tops from the vegetables. She put the green tops in a basket. "Goats love fresh green tops," she said to Andrewshek, as she put the basket on the back porch by the door. She left the door wide open.

The naughty white goat was peeping over the roof to see what she could see. She saw the green tops in the basket by the kitchen door. Immediately she felt very hungry. She clambered down from the roof. She stole up to the basket.

"Well! well!" laughed Andrewshek's Auntie Katushka, as she slipped a halter around the white goat's neck. "We soon shall have plenty of milk for our poppy seed cakes."

Mr. Groundhog Turns Around

By JAMES T. BRADY

Helen
Prickett

A drop of icy water fell right on Mr. Groundhog's nose. His nose twitched, but he went on sleeping. Plop! Another drop landed in the same place. This time Mr. Groundhog opened his eyes. At first he couldn't remember where he was, he had been sleeping so long and so soundly. But then he recognized the inside of his home, and he reached over to where his wife was snoring peacefully. "Time to wake up!" he called as he shook her. "Wake up!"

Mrs. Groundhog raised her head just a little. "What's the matter?"

"Spring's the matter, that's what!" declared Mr. Groundhog. "Look at the water coming into our house!"

Mrs. Groundhog sat up and looked around. Sure enough, big drops of water were coming through the roof and dripping down on the floor. At sight of this, Mrs. Groundhog woke up completely, jumped out of bed, scurried for her maple-leaf mop, and went to work mopping up the puddles.

"The snow must be melting outside," Mr. Groundhog said.
"Maybe you're right," his wife admitted. "What day is it,
anyway?"

Mr. Groundhog waddled over to the groundhog calendar,
his tail trailing behind him. "It must be February second," he
announced. "We've been asleep since November. I'm tired of
being indoors so long."

"I'll bet it's still cold outside, though," Mrs. Groundhog said.

"Nonsense!" answered her husband. "You can see the sunlight shining at the door." Mr. Groundhog pointed down one of the passages leading to the outdoors. "Besides," he added, patting his stomach with a furry paw, "I'm starved. I could eat a whole field of nice red clover."

"Don't get too excited about food," warned Mrs. Groundhog. "It's probably too early in the year to find anything to eat."

Mr. Groundhog didn't answer. He was already halfway down the tunnel where he saw the sunlight. As he came closer to the entrance, the air was much colder. He shivered a little and said to himself,

Helen
Prickett

"It *is* a bit chilly!" But then he thought of the sweet red clover which might be waiting for him in the fields outside. He hurried on. When he reached the outside, an icy blast nipped his nose, but he said stubbornly, "Ah, this fresh air smells good. Spring is here!"

He put his head out of the hole, then one paw and then another, until he was completely out of the tunnel. There was plenty of sunshine, to be sure, but the air was cold, and Mr. Groundhog's paws were freezing on the hard snow underfoot. He couldn't see a sign of clover, or, for that matter, of anything green. He faced the sun, and this warmed his nose but did not reach his tail, which felt very, very cold. "I'd better turn around," he remarked to himself, and turned his back to the sun. He waved his tail to and fro, searching the ground for just one little bit of green grass.

Then suddenly he saw something close to him that made every hair on his body stand on end! Quick as lightning Mr. Groundhog scampered back into his hole.

"My goodness!" exclaimed Mrs. Groundhog. "Whatever is the matter with you?"

But Mr. Groundhog was so frightened that when he opened his mouth to answer her, not a sound came out.

"Was it a fox?" asked Mrs. Groundhog. "Was it a weasel?"

Still Mr. Groundhog didn't answer. He just shook his head. "Well, what was it?"

Helen
Prickett

Finally Mr. Ground-
hog found his voice
and said, "We might
as well go back to sleep
for a few more weeks."
And so saying, he
crawled into bed, curled up in a ball and went fast asleep.

"I guess I may as well have another nap myself," said Mrs.
Groundhog, yawning, "But I do wonder what it could have
been that frightened my husband?"

Do *you* know what it was?

Whisky Frisky

Whisky Frisky,
Hippity-hop
Up he goes
To the treetop!

Whirly, twirly,
Round and round,
Down he scampers
To the ground.

Furly, curly,
What a tail!
Tall as a feather,
Broad as a sail!

Where's his supper?
In the shell,
Snap, cracky,
Out it fell.

Author Unknown

129

The Butterbean Tent

All through the garden I went and went,
And I walked in under the butterbean tent.

The poles leaned up like a good tepee
And made a nice little house for me.

I had a hard brown clod for a seat,
And all outside was a cool green street.

A little green worm and a butterfly
And a cricket-like thing that could hop went by.

Hidden away there were flocks and flocks
Of bugs that could go like little clocks.

Such a good day it was when I spent
A long, long while in the butterbean tent.

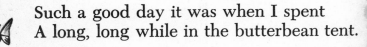

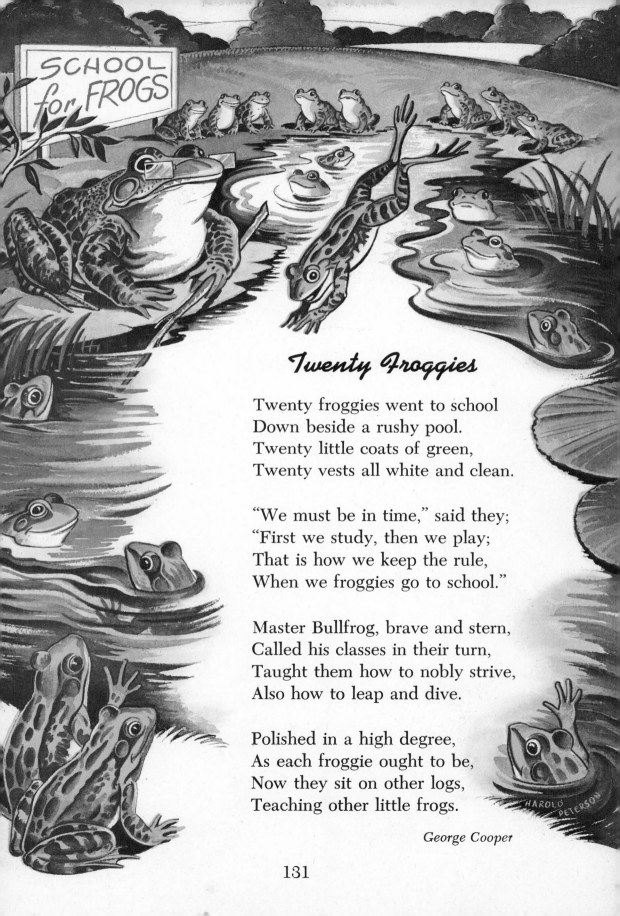

Twenty Froggies

Twenty froggies went to school
Down beside a rushy pool.
Twenty little coats of green,
Twenty vests all white and clean.

"We must be in time," said they;
"First we study, then we play;
That is how we keep the rule,
When we froggies go to school."

Master Bullfrog, brave and stern,
Called his classes in their turn,
Taught them how to nobly strive,
Also how to leap and dive.

Polished in a high degree,
As each froggie ought to be,
Now they sit on other logs,
Teaching other little frogs.

George Cooper

131

Baby Seeds

In a milkweed cradle,
Snug and warm,
Baby seeds are hiding,
Safe from harm.
Open wide the cradle,
Hold it high!
Come Mr. Wind,
Help them fly.

Author Unknown

132

Jan Ross

Angus and the Ducks

By MARJORIE FLACK

Once there was a very young little dog whose name was Angus, because his mother and his father came from Scotland.

Although the rest of Angus was quite small, his head was very large and so were his feet.

Angus was curious about many places and many things:

He was curious about WHAT lived under the sofa and in dark corners and

WHO was the little dog in the mirror.

He was curious about Things-Which-Come-Apart and those Things-Which-Don't-Come-Apart; such as SLIPPERS and Gentlemen's SUSPENDERS and things like that.

Angus was also curious about Things-Outdoors but he could not find out much about them because of a leash.

The leash was fastened at one end to the collar around his neck and at the other end to SOMEBODY ELSE.

But Angus was most curious of all about a NOISE which came from the OTHER SIDE of the large green hedge at the end of the garden.

The noise usually sounded like this:
Quack! Quack! Quackety! Quack!!!
But sometimes it sounded like this:
Quackety! Quackety! Quackety! Quack!!

Jan Ross

One day the door between OUTDOORS and INDOORS was left open by mistake; and out went Angus without the leash or SOMEBODY ELSE.

Down the little path he ran until he came to the large green hedge at the end of the garden.

He tried to go around it but it was much too long. He tried to go over it but it was much too high. So Angus went under the large green hedge . . . . . .

and came out on the OTHER SIDE. There, directly in front of him were two white DUCKS. They were marching forward one-foot-up and one-foot-down. Quack! Quack! Quackety! Quack!!!

Angus said, WOO-OOF!!!

Away went the DUCKS all of a flutter. Quackety! Quackety! Quackety! Quackety! Quackety!!!

Angus followed after.

Soon the DUCKS stopped by a stone watering trough under a mulberry tree.

Angus stopped, too. Each DUCK dipped a yellow bill in the clear cool water. Angus watched. Each DUCK took a long drink of the cool clear water. Still Angus watched. Each DUCK took another long drink of cool clear water. Then Angus said:

WOO-OO-OOF!!!

Away the DUCKS scuttled and
Angus lapped the clear cool water.
Birds sang in the mulberry tree.
The Sun made patterns through
the leaves over the grass.

The DUCKS talked together: Quack! Quack! Quack! Then:

HISS-S-S-S-S-S-S!!!

HISS-S-S-S-S-S-S!!!

The first DUCK nipped Angus's tail!
HISS-S-S-S-S-S-S!!!

HISS-S-S-S-S-S-S!!!
The second DUCK flapped her wings!

Angus scrambled under the large green hedge,

scurried up the little path,

scampered into the house

and crawled under the sofa.

For exactly THREE minutes

by the clock, Angus was

NOT curious about anything at all.

How Creatures Move

The lion walks on padded paws,

The squirrel leaps from limb to limb,

While flies can crawl straight up a wall,

And seals can dive and swim.

The worm, he wiggles all around,

The monkey swings by his tail,

And birds may hop upon the ground,

Or spread their wings and sail.

But boys and girls have much more fun;

They leap and dance

And walk and run.

Author Unknown

Come, Little Leaves

"Come little leaves," said the wind one day,
"Come o'er the meadows with me and play;
Put on your dresses of red and gold,
For summer is gone and the days grow cold."

Soon as the leaves heard the wind's loud call,
Down they came fluttering, one and all;
Over the brown fields they danced and flew,
Singing the glad little songs they knew.

146

"Cricket, good-by. We've been friends so long;
Little brook, sing us your farewell song;
Say you are sorry to see us go;
Ah, you will miss us, right well we know."

Dancing and whirling, the little leaves went;
Winter had called them, and they were content;
Soon, fast asleep in their earthy beds,
The snow laid a coverlid over their heads.

George Cooper

HAROLD PETERSON

How Did He Do It

EMILIE POULSSON

There was once a boy who had three goats.

All day long the three goats ran and played upon the hill. At night the boy drove them home.

One night the frisky things jumped into a turnip field. He could not get them out.

Then the boy sat down on the hillside and cried.

As he sat there a hare came along.

"Why do you cry?" asked the hare.

"I cry because I cannot get the goats out of the field," said the boy.

"I'll do it," said the hare.

So he tried, but the goats would not come.

Then the hare, too, sat down and cried.

148

Along came a fox. "Why do you cry?" asked the fox.

"I am crying because the boy cries," said the hare. "The boy is crying because he cannot get three goats out of the turnip field."

"I'll do it," said the fox.

So the fox tried to get them out of the field. But the goats would not come.

Then the fox, too, began to cry.

Soon after a wolf came along.

"Why do you cry?" asked the wolf.

"I am crying because the hare cries," said the fox. "The hare cries because the boy cries. The boy cries because he cannot get the three goats out of the turnip field."

"I'll do it," said the wolf.

He tried, but the goats would not leave the turnip field.

So he sat down with the others and began to cry, too.

After a little, a bee flew over the hill and saw them all sitting there, crying.

"Why do you cry?" said the bee to the wolf.

"I am crying because the fox cries. The fox is crying because the hare cries. The hare cries because the boy cries. The boy cries because he cannot get the goats out of the turnip field."

"I'll do it," said the bee.

Then the big animals and the boy stopped crying a moment to laugh at the tiny bee.

But the bee flew away into the turnip field and alighted upon one of the goats, and said:

"Buz-z-z-z-z!"

And out ran the goats, every one!

Mrs. Snipkin and Mrs. Wobblechin

Skinny Mrs. Snipkin,
With her little pipkin,
Sat by the fireside a-warming of her toes.
Fat Mrs. Wobblechin,
With her little doublechin,
Sat by the window a-cooling of her nose.

Says this one to that one,
"Oh! you silly fat one,
Will you shut the window down?
You're freezing me to death!"
Says that one to t'other one,
"Good gracious, how you bother one!
There isn't air enough for me
to draw my precious breath!"

Skinny Mrs. Snipkin,
Took her little pipkin,
Threw it straight across the room
as hard as she could throw;
Hit Mrs. Wobblechin
On her little doublechin,
And out of the window
a-tumble she did go.

Laura E. Richards

The Sprinkler

The sprinkler is what's fun to see
Underneath our big elm tree.

It whirls around its big wet drops,
First on my mother's pretty phlox
And last on father's hollyhocks.

And all their little faces get
So very, very nice and wet.

And when no one is there to see
I run and get some drops on me.

Dorothy Aldis

Jane Scott

The Ice-Cream Man

When summer's in the city,
　And brick's a blaze of heat,
The Ice-Cream Man with his little cart
　Goes trundling down the street.

　Beneath his round umbrella,
　　Oh, what a joyful sight,
　To see him fill the cones with mounds
　　Of cooling brown or white:

　　Vanilla, chocolate, strawberry,
　　　Or chilly things to drink
　　From bottles full of frosty-fizz,
　　　Green, orange, white, or pink.

　　　His cart might be a flower bed
　　　　Of roses and sweet peas,
　　　The way the children cluster round
　　　　As thick as honeybees.

Rachel Field

Falling Snow

See the pretty snowflakes
    Falling from the sky;
On the walk and housetop
    Soft and thick they lie.

On the window-ledges
    On the branches bare;
Now how fast they gather,
    Filling all the air.

Look into the garden,
    Where the grass was green;
Covered by the snowflakes,
    Not a blade is seen.

Now the bare black bushes
    All look soft and white,
Every twig is laden—
    What a pretty sight!

Author Unknown

The Playhouse Key

This is the key to the playhouse
    In the woods by the pebbly shore,
It's winter now; I wonder if
    There's snow about the door?

I wonder if the fir trees tap
    Green fingers on the pane
If sea gulls cry and the roof is wet
    And tinkley with rain?

I wonder if the flower-sprigged cups
    And plates sit on their shelf,
And if my little painted chair
    Is rocking by itself?

Rachel Field

155

Farewell to the Farm

The coach is at the door at last;
The eager children, mounting fast
And kissing hands, in chorus sing:
"Good-bye, good-bye, to everything!

"To house and garden, field and lawn,
The meadow-gates we swang upon,
To pump and stable, tree and swing,
Good-bye, good-bye, to everything!

"And fare you well for evermore,
O ladder at the hayloft door,
O hayloft where the cobwebs cling,
Good-bye, good-bye, to everything!"

Crack goes the whip, and off we go;
The trees and houses smaller grow;
Last, round the woody turn we swing:
"Good-bye, good-bye, to everything!"

Robert Louis Stevenson

Mr. Apple Names the Children

By JEAN McDEVITT

Mr. and Mrs. Apple lived in the city. They lived in a little apartment in a big apartment house. They had lived there a long time. When Mr. and Mrs. Apple first went to live in the city there were not any little Apples. Now there were five little Apples.

The oldest Apple boy was named MacIntosh. This was Mr. Apple's idea. He said there was no use having a name like Apple if you just called your children by ordinary names. "George Apple or Tom Apple or Jack Apple would not do at all," said Mr. Apple. So the Apple children were named for real apples.

Ann

Snow

Delia

Mac

Jon

Mrs. Apple did not like this idea of Mr. Apple's very much.

"MacIntosh is much too big a name for a tiny baby," said Mrs. Apple.

"He will not be a tiny baby long," said Mr. Apple. "We will call him Mac for short."

Mrs. Apple saw that Mr. Apple wanted very much to call the baby Mac-Intosh. "Very well," said Mrs. Apple. "We will call him Mac." She knew she could not have her own way all the time. Mr. Apple must sometimes have what he wanted. So when the second little Apple came he was named Jonathan. He was called Jon for short.

Mrs. Apple got used to the idea of MacIntosh and Jonathan for her two boys. She even boasted a little bit to her neighbors.

"Mr. Apple is very clever," Mrs. Apple would say. "He has such fine ideas. No one but a man as clever as Mr. Apple would have thought of naming his children for real apples."

Then the first little girl came along. It was much harder for Mr. Apple to think of an apple name for a little girl.

"If she had been a boy," said Mr. Apple, "I could have named her Spitzenberg. She could have been Spitz for short."

"She is not a boy and she cannot be named Spitzenberg," said Mrs. Apple. "A little girl should have a pretty name. She cannot be called Spitz."

"How would Delicious be?" asked Mr. Apple. "There is a fine apple named Delicious."

"Delicious is a beautiful name," said Mrs. Apple happily. "I think we will call her Delia for short."

The fourth little Apple was also a girl. Mr. Apple had a very hard time indeed to find an apple name for her. He thought and thought about it. But he could not think of an apple name for another little girl.

One day Mr. Apple said to Mrs. Apple, "I know what I will do. I will go to the library and look for a name in a book."

"In a book!" said Mrs. Apple. "Is there a book with apple names in it?"

"Yes," said Mr. Apple. "I am sure there is. There is a book for everything in the library."

So Mr. Apple went to the public library. He said to the Librarian, "Have you a book that will tell me the names of apples?"

"Yes indeed," said the Librarian. "We have a Garden Encyclopedia."

Mr. Apple took the big book and sat down at a table. He hunted and hunted through it for an apple name for his second little girl. He wrote many names on a piece of paper. Then he took the Garden Encyclopedia back to the Librarian.

"Thank you for your help," said Mr. Apple.

"Did you find what you wanted?" asked the Librarian.

"Well," said Mr. Apple, "I found a great many names, but they are not very good names for a little girl."

The Librarian looked very surprised. "I thought you wanted names of apples," she said.

"So I did, so I did," answered Mr. Apple.

He did not stop to explain. He wanted to get home. He wanted to see if Mrs. Apple would like any of the names he had found.

"Did you find a book of apple names?" asked Mrs. Apple, as soon as Mr. Apple came home.

"Oh yes," said Mr. Apple. "There is a big, big book of apple names in the library. It is called a Garden Encyclopedia."

"It was very clever of you to think of going to the library, Mr. Apple," said Mrs. Apple.

"That is what a library is for," said Mr. Apple.

"What names did you find?" asked Mrs. Apple anxiously.

"Well," said Mr. Apple, "that is the trouble. There were many fine apple names for little boys. If she were a boy, we could call her Fall Pippin or Baldwin. I am very fond of Baldwin apples," said Mr. Apple. "If she were only a boy I would name her Baldwin. We could call her Baldy for short."

"She is not a boy," said Mrs. Apple. "And she cannot be called Baldwin. She cannot be called Baldy. She is a sweet little girl. I am glad she is a little girl. I like little girls."

"I like little girls, too," said Mr. Apple. "But it is so hard to find good names for them."

Mrs. Apple did not say that of course the baby could be called Nancy or Mary or Elizabeth. She did not want to hurt Mr. Apple's feelings.

"What were some of the other names in the Garden Encyclopedia?" asked Mrs. Apple.

"There is an apple called a Snow Apple," said Mr. Apple.

"Snow Apple," said Mrs. Apple. "Snow Apple," she said again. "That is very pretty. I think we will name the baby Snow. She will not need a nickname."

Mr. Apple was very pleased that Mrs. Apple liked one of the names he had found. Snow was a good name for the baby. She had very white skin and bright red cheeks. She looked very much like a little round snow apple. Mr. and Mrs. Apple were very happy to have found just the right name for the fourth little Apple.

After a while the fifth little Apple came. The fifth little Apple was a girl, too! Poor Mr. Apple was quite upset again.

"Oh, dear, oh, dear," he said. "I cannot possibly think of another apple name for a little girl."

"Why not go to the library again?" asked Mrs. Apple.

"No, it would not do any good," said Mr. Apple. "I wrote

down all the apple names there were in the Garden Encyclopedia. There was not another name for a little girl."

"Well," said Mrs. Apple, "four of our children have apple names. Why not just name this one Nancy or Mary or Elizabeth?"

"No, no," said Mr. Apple. "Those names will not do for an Apple child. I do wish I could think of an apple name for another little girl."

"There!" said Mrs. Apple in excitement. "An Apple — An Apple."

Mr. Apple looked at Mrs. Apple in great surprise.

"What do you mean by saying an apple over and over again?" he asked.

"Why, don't you see?" replied Mrs. Apple. "We can call the fifth baby An Apple. We will spell it An-n. Ann Apple is her name."

Now Mr. Apple saw that Mrs. Apple wanted very much to call the little girl Ann. He did not like this idea of Mrs. Apple's so very much. But Mr. Apple knew that he could not always have what he wanted. Mrs. Apple must sometimes have what she wanted. So Mr. Apple said,

"Ann Apple is not a bad name. At least it makes sense. Nancy Apple or Mary Apple or Elizabeth Apple would not make sense at all."

So the fifth and last little Apple had a real little girl's name, and that pleased Mrs. Apple very much indeed.

On the Trail of the Mad Moose

By AUDREY McKIM

Leonard

It started out as a very quiet Saturday. Gary and Bruce were sitting on the back porch trying to decide how to spend the morning when they saw one of their neighbors, Mrs. Mc-Crum, running down the street.

"Mad moose!" Mrs. McCrum screamed as she ran past the house, waving a tea towel over her head.

Gary and Bruce leaped to their feet. A mad moose! With a shout they ran after Mrs. McCrum. "Where is it? Where is it?" they cried, as they caught up with the neighbor.

Mrs. McCrum was almost out of breath, and she had slowed down to a walking pace now, but she answered without stopping. "It just went across my yard—and took most of my clothesline with it!" she panted. "Mad as a hatter it was!"

"What makes you think it is mad?" asked Bruce, running beside Mrs. McCrum while his eyes darted about in every direction. The town of Jasper looked as peaceful as always. He could see some deer walking down Patricia Street, but then deer were very tame and always a common sight in the National Park.

"Why do I think the moose is mad?" gasped Mrs. McCrum. "It went snorting and puffing and blowing through the garden, and nothing would stop it. I tell you, it is a dangerous thing to have in town! Someone should tell the police!" She began to run again, her two feet pounding down the road.

Bruce and Gary leaped forward and began to outstrip Mrs. McCrum. Mothers and children came running from the houses as the boys called, "Mad moose! Mad moose!"

Around the corner they came upon two tourists who had just been thrown into a patch of newly planted grass. The two tourists' horses were galloping off toward the other end of the town. Gary and Bruce helped the two tourists  to their feet and brushed them off. The tourists looked as if they were not quite sure what had happened to them. "I think it was a moose!" gasped one.

"It came right toward us, and our horses reared up!" the second tourist explained breathlessly.

"It's a mad moose," explained Gary. "It took Mrs. McCrum's clothesline right off the poles."

"A mad moose!" the two tourists exclaimed. "How dreadful!"

By this time, quite a big crowd had collected. For a minute everybody talked at once, and then someone pointed down the street and shouted, "What's happened to Mr. Meadow's milk wagon?"

The crowd stared. There stood Mr. Meadow in a welter of milk and broken bottles. His wagon had been pushed over to one side of the road, and Snooze, his old horse, was getting up from a kneeling position.

Bruce, Gary, Mrs. McCrum and all the other people stopped talking and hurried toward the milkman.

"I give up!" shouted Mr. Meadow. "I give up, I tell you! Things have come to a pretty pass when a fellow can't come in to town without his horse being stampeded by a wild moose! Somebody get the police!"

"Which way did the moose go?" asked Mrs. McCrum.

"That way," Mr. Meadow answered, as he pointed toward Whistler Mountain. Before he could say anything more, the crowd rushed past him.

"Guess you and I had better join the mob, Snooze," the milkman said to his horse. "We owe that moose a thing or two!"

Soon old Snooze was out of the harness and galloping after the crowd, with Mr. Meadow on his back.

On by the church and across the schoolyard. And then Gary and Bruce saw the moose. It was running, with blowing nostrils, straight toward the unfenced ball park, where some girls were having a game of softball.

"Mad moose!" screamed Mrs. McCrum and all the others in the pursuing crowd.

The girls turned their startled faces toward the noise and saw the big moose charging down upon them. With loud screams, they ran toward the bleachers, their bats and ball forgotten.

"Where are the police?" demanded Mrs. McCrum in a loud voice. "Has anyone called them?"

Apparently no one had, for there were no officers in sight. Everybody had been so busy chasing the moose that no one had taken time to call up and report the case at police headquarters.

Now the moose circled the ball field, snorting and pawing the ground. Then suddenly it stood still!

The crowd grew hushed. What would happen next? The moose lifted its head. Its ears twitched and became still. Then, in the breathless quiet, a rustle was seen in the underbrush by the roadside. All eyes turned toward the spot, as a spindly young moose tottered out of the ditch and moved toward the center of the ball field.

Now the big moose let out a strange cry and rushed forward. It pressed a large and loving nose against the calf, and then, with that same nose, gave the baby moose a firm push in the direction of the woods. The two of them moved slowly into the forest, and then were seen no more.

"Well!" said one of the two tourists. "It wasn't a mad moose, after all!"

"Just a mother moose looking for her lost baby," said Mrs. McCrum. "And such a commotion as we have all made!"

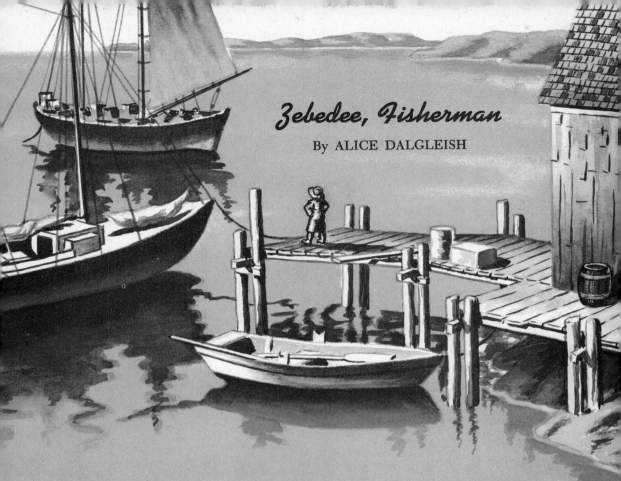

Zebedee, Fisherman

By ALICE DALGLEISH

Zebedee lived in a fishing village in Nova Scotia. His home was a white house by the edge of the sea.

When he was not in school or asleep, there were two places where Zebedee could be found. One was the old, white boat on the beach just below his own cottage. The other was the wharf where the fishing boats came and went. It was on the Bay of Fundy, just half a mile over the hill.

Everyone knew Zebedee because of his wide, cheerful smile and his very blue eyes. They were even bluer than the Bay of Fundy, and that is very blue indeed.

When people first met him they would say, "Zebedee! What a strange name for a little boy!"

Zebedee did not mind having a strange name, because in the first place everyone called him Zeb, and in the second place his mother had explained to him exactly how he happened to have that name. This is the story:

When Zebedee was born he was the only child in the family, so, of course, all the aunts and uncles and grandparents wanted to have something to say about his name. The aunts suggested "Earl" and "Everard" and "Leslie." The uncles suggested "John" and "Thomas" and "Richard." The baby's mother did not care for any of these, nor did the baby's father. There was so much discussion over the naming of this blue-eyed scrap of a baby that when the time came to take him to the church to be baptized nothing had been decided. This was serious. The minister was waiting and there was the baby in his long, white, embroidered christening robe. What was to be done about it?

"There is only one thing we can do," said Grandfather Harris. He sat and took the family Bible on his knees. "The first name at which the Book opens shall be the child's."

Grandfather Harris put on his spectacles, opened the Bible, and ran his finger down the page. The aunts and the baby's mother held their breath, hoping the name would not be "Ezekiel" or "Methuselah." Grandfather Harris cleared his throat. "It is a good name for a fisherman's son, for it was the name of a fisherman," he said. "The name is 'Zebedee'."

Perhaps it was because of his name that Zebedee wished so much to be a fisherman. He loved the sea; he loved boats and fishing lines and rubber boots. He thought there was nothing in the world so interesting and exciting. It was interesting and exciting all the year round—spring, summer, and autumn.

In the spring it was lobster fishing.

All winter long there was a fence of lobster pots at one side of Zeb's house. In the spring, Zeb's father piled the lobster pots onto an oxcart and jogged slowly up to the Bay of Fundy. Zeb rode on the cart while his father walked. Up the hill they went, past Miss Letty's house, and down the steep hill to the wharf. The oxen were so strong and surefooted they did not seem to mind the heavy load or the rough road.

When the lobster pots were loaded on the boats, Zeb's father and the fishermen pushed off, leaving him on the wharf.

"Lobster fishing is too cold for little boys," they said.

Zeb went home slowly and sadly.

In the summer Zebedee was almost always on the wharf, but the fishermen would not take him out with them.

"Little boys are a nuisance in boats," they said.

So Zeb watched the boats go out and walked on the wharf among the piles of cod that lay drying in the sun. Sometimes the men would let him help to pile the dried fish into neat little rounded stacks, fish on fish, tail to tail.

When the fishing boats came in, Zeb thought there was nothing more exciting than to help unload the silvery cod and

haddock, mackerel, and pollock. When the fish were unloaded, Zeb and his father walked home, their rubber boots all covered with glistening scales, their rubber coats smelling of fish.

On autumn evenings Zeb was sometimes allowed to stay up late and watch the fishermen drive the herring from Saint Mary's Bay into the Cove. Back and forth on the water darted the fishing boats, each with a flaming torch at the bow. The herring came straight for the flares, and soon the Cove was full of tiny fish, leaping from the water.

Zeb could scarcely stay on the wharf; he longed to have a net and scoop the herring into the boats. The fishermen would not take him out with them.

"It is dangerous for little boys when we have a torch in the boat," they said.

"It's always dangerous for little boys," said Zeb, sadly.

At last, when Zeb was seven years old, his father took him fishing. Zeb had to wake up very early. He put on two pairs of stockings, two sweaters, and over the sweaters his rubber coat. Last of all he put on his mittens, which were white, as a fisherman's mittens must be. It was quite difficult to walk up the hill to the Bay of Fundy in all those clothes. The morning was cold and it was still almost dark. Zeb began to wonder if he really wanted to be a fisherman.

As the boat pushed off from the wharf, Zeb began to feel more cheerful. When they were out in the bay and Zeb's own line slipped through his fingers into the dark, chilly water, he forgot all about the cold. When his first fish, a big silver cod, lay in the bottom of the boat, there was no happier boy in any fishing village from Sandy Cove to Tiverton.

Now fogs come in suddenly on Fundy, and before the fishermen knew it, a thick, white fog had blotted out the land. There was no beach to be seen, no bluffs; even the wharf had vanished from sight. Perhaps they were opposite the wharf—perhaps they were nearer the wicked rocks just off the point.

They drifted, waiting for the fog to clear. The boat bobbed up and down on the water, and Zeb began to feel queer. His hands were cold, but he said nothing. He was sure it was hours before the fog lifted enough for them to see. Then the surprising thing was that they were only a few yards from the end of the wharf! How good the sturdy gray piles looked to Zeb! By the time he had climbed the ladder at the side of the wharf, and started up the hill, he began to feel better, though his head was dizzy and his legs were shaky. In his right hand Zeb carried the big silver cod, in his left hand a large pollock. His rubber boots were covered with glittering fish scales.

At the top of the hill Zeb and his father met Miss Letty's twins coming back from the village.

"Look!" said Zeb, holding up his fish. Abigail and Sara looked, and agreed that they were the finest fish that had ever come out of the Bay of Fundy.

Farther down the hill, they met Miranda Saunders with a white kitten tucked under her arm. Miranda did not say a word, but Zeb knew that she wished she could go fishing.

When they reached the little house by the Cove, Zeb's mother was at the gate watching for him. A refreshing smell of dinner came through the front door. Zeb's mother admired the silver cod and the fine pollock.

"Weren't you afraid, out there in the fog?" she asked.

"No!" said Zebedee.

"Weren't you cold?"

"Not a bit!" said Zebedee, though his hands were blue.

"Or seasick?"

"Of course not" — although the ground on which he stood had a curious way of coming up to meet him.

There was not the least doubt that Zebedee was a fisherman!

First Thanksgiving of All

Peace and Mercy and Jonathan,
And Patience (very small),
Stood by the table giving thanks
The first Thanksgiving of all.
There was very little for them to eat,
Nothing special and nothing sweet;
Only bread and a little broth,
And a bit of fruit
   (and no tablecloth);
But Peace and Mercy and Jonathan
And Patience, in a row,
Stood up and asked a blessing on
Thanksgiving, long ago.

186

Thankful they were their ship had come
Safely across the sea;
Thankful for hearth and home,
And kin and company;
They were glad of broth to go with their bread,
Glad their apples were round and red,
Glad of mayflowers they would bring
Out of the woods again next spring.
So Peace and Mercy and Jonathan,
And Patience (very small),
Stood up gratefully giving thanks
The first Thanksgiving of all.

Nancy Byrd Turner

187

Santa Claus

Little fairy snowflakes
  Dancing in the flue;
Old Mr. Santa Claus,
  What is keeping you?
Twilight and firelight
  Shadows come and go;
Merry chime of sleighbells
  Twinkling through the snow.
Mother's knitting stockings,
  Pussy's got the ball.
Don't you think that Christmas
  Is pleasantest of all?

Author Unknown

188

Old Christmas Carol

God bless the master of this house,
  Likewise the mistress too,
And all the little children,
  That round the table go,
And all your kin and kinsmen
  That dwell both far and near;
I wish you a Merry Christmas,
  And a Happy New Year.

Author Unknown

What My Little Brother Thinks!

My little brother is—oh, so funny!
He thinks that a king is made of money,
He thinks little cherubs, overhead,
Hold up the stars to light us to bed.

He thinks little fairies make the clamor
In Grandpa's watch, with a tiny hammer.
He thinks that fairies live in a book,
Or can dance in kettles to frighten Cook.

He thinks the grasshoppers bring molasses,
That a fairy over the bright moon passes.
He thinks my Jack-in-the-box is alive;—
But my little brother is only five.

But the best of all, he is really certain
He once saw Santa Claus through the curtain;
And he thinks Old Santa'll come by and by
On Christmas Eve—and so do I!

Author Unknown

190

Jan Ross

Long, Long Ago

Winds through the olive trees
   Softly did blow,
Round little Bethlehem
   Long, long ago.

Sheep on the hillside lay
   Whiter than snow;
Shepherds were watching them,
   Long, long ago.

Then from the happy sky,
   Angels bent low,
Singing their songs of joy,
   Long, long ago.

For in a manger bed,
   Cradled we know,
Christ came to Bethlehem,
   Long, long ago.

Author Unknown

Jan Ross

Picture-Books in Winter

Summer fading, winter comes—
Frosty mornings, tingling thumbs,
Window robins, winter rooks,
And the picture story-books.

Water now is turned to stone
Nurse and I can walk upon;
Still we find the flowing brooks
In the picture story-books.

All the pretty things put by,
Wait upon the children's eye,
Sheep and shepherds, trees and crooks,
In the picture story-books.

We may see how all things are,
Seas and cities, near and far,
And the flying fairies' looks,
In the picture story-books.

How am I to sing your praise,
Happy chimney-corner days,
Sitting safe in nursery nooks,
Reading picture story-books?

Robert Louis Stevenson